Beyond the Frozen Forest

Sandy Broome
Illustrated by Alan Capps

ISBN: 148001236X
ISBN-13: 9781480012363

To
Ava Grace, Lilia Carolyn, Cadence Louise,
Steven Pate & Anderson Glenn
and any future children who call me Nana
~I love you from here to heaven and back~

Deep in a forest one snowy day,
a boy who lived all alone
decided to build some snowmen,
so he would have friends of his own.

He took a deep breath of the frosty air—
so cold that it cut like a knife;
and with one great puff blew a magical cloud
that brought the snow children to life.

Each day until it was dark outside,
the boy and his friends laughed and played.
Sharing, exploring, and having fun,
they were safe in the forest's cool shade.

Days there were practically perfect,
and nights were equally grand!
The boy loved his friends and the joys they shared
in their icy wonderland.

Beyond the frozen forest,
a troll watched the snow children play.
Hearing their giggles and seeing their glee
made him grumpy and angry that day.

Each day the troll grew more jealous
of the snow children and the boy.
And with all of his might, he hated the sight
of their happiness, love and joy.

Day after day he paced and planned,
knowing and believing—
that he could trick them by telling a lie.
He was very good at deceiving!

One day in the beautiful forest, the troll paid the children a visit. "Hello my dears, I'm new around here. This place is truly exquisite!"

The snow children gathered around
to hear what the troll had to say.
"Yes, this place is fine, but it isn't the best,
I know of a great place to play!"

The troll described a meadow
with colorful, festive flowers,
where rolling hills and sunny skies
meant playtime could last for hours!

He made their forest seem boring.
The meadow would be much more fun.
So they ran down the hill toward the beautiful field
as fast as their snow feet could run.

When the boy returned his friends were gone.
The troll had lured them away!
He'd promised them thrills, excitement, delights,
adventure and fun every day.

So, how could the boy convince them
that leaving their forest's safe shade
to follow the troll would be deadly?
A rescuing plan must be made!

What would help them understand?
What might help them see?
"I'll become one of them!" the boy announced.
"Then maybe they'll listen to me!"

When the boy was fully covered
with the purest, whitest snow,
there was not a minute left to spare—
the snow boy had to go!

Yes, leaving the frozen forest,
meant risking that he might melt, too.
But he loved his friends with all of his heart,
so what else was the brave boy to do?

He found his friends in the sunshine
melting as they played--
but they paid him no attention.
No, they did not miss the shade.

"Come home with me to the forest,"
the snow boy invited each one.
But the snow children kept on playing.
The meadow was far too much fun!

The delighted old troll furrowed his brow,
and rubbed his prickly chin.
"Let's teach that snow boy a lesson," he snarled
with a devious, dastardly grin.

"I have a thousand snowballs!
They're big and icy and round!
And if you throw them hard enough
you'll knock that snow boy down!"

The snow children jeered at the snow boy
as they pelted and pummeled and threw--
shouting, "Leave us alone, we don't want to go home!"
But the boy sighed, "I still love all of you…"

They didn't hear him speak of his love,
Their shouts were much too loud.
And the hateful old troll was as pleased as could be,
in fact, you might say he was proud.

Silence came next; they couldn't believe
that the snow boy's life had ended.
"Let's celebrate!" said the wicked troll,
"It's exactly as I intended!"

Hot, blazing sunshine was beaming,
it seemed that the sky was on fire!
As they melted away on that darkest of days
they could see now, the troll was a liar.

For two long days the heat of the sun
helped to uncover the grave
of the boy, who disguised as a snowman,
had been so caring and brave.

The third morning's dawn was majestic,
and much to their startled surprise
the snow that had covered the snow boy was gone!
They hardly believed their own eyes!

Up from his snow grave their old friend arose,
a miracle happened that day!
But just as he'd warned them, just as he'd feared—
his snow friends were melting away.

The snow children couldn't contain their joy—
might this be their second chance?
Their hearts were almost afraid to hope
but their snow feet just wanted to dance!

The troll was displeased and disgruntled.
His plans had fallen apart.
As he shuffled away it was quite clear that day
that really the troll had no heart.

"Will you take us back to your forest?"
the snow children asked their friend.
With deep love in his heart he pointed the way
to the place where *real* life has no end.

At last the snow children understood,
no price for their lives was too great.
Their friend had selflessly offered his life
to save them from death's cruel fate.

If you ask the snow children they'll tell you the truth,
life in the forest is grand.
The snow boy was gracious to save each of them
from the terrible thing that troll planned.

They'll say each new day's like a present now—
tied up with a ribbon called joy!
And the light that fills up the forest
is love's glow from the face of the boy.

~ *the end.* ~

Dear Mom, Dad, Grandparent, Aunt, Uncle, Friend, Babysitter, Reader, The bestselling book of all time is the Bible. A compilation of sixty-six separate books that are woven together like the finest tapestry, the sacred scriptures present in vivid detail the account of God's amazing, redemptive plan for his children.

In Genesis, the Bible's first book, we learn that God created people with the intention of protecting them and providing for their every need. This same God was gracious enough, loving enough and wise enough to allow the people he made to choose whether to stay in that wonderful place or go their own way.

As you may know, God's children listened to "the troll" (actually he was a serpent in Genesis) and found themselves living in the world's "meadow," where not only fun, but also suffering, and ultimately death, would result.

God could have chosen to leave them in the meadow without hope.

Instead, he planned their rescue through an indescribable act of love and grace. He became one of them! God sent his only Son, Jesus Christ, to rescue and redeem his children. And they (we) responded by killing him.

What the story you've just read did not convey is that the rescuing savior *WILLINGLY* died, and in doing so, he paid God's required price for his children's disobedient decision to leave the "forest" and wander astray. The rescuer selflessly gave up his life to save all who would trust him as their *forgiver and leader*, offering the promise of unbroken friendship and everlasting fellowship to all who would return.

Are you still living "beyond the frozen forest?" If so, he wants me to invite you to come home.

soli Deo gloria!
Sandy ∾

to learn more about this story log on to
www.beyondthefrozenforest.com

Made in the USA
Columbia, SC
19 September 2019